Special thanks to:

Hanna Richards (editor) and Stephen Stone (illustrator and book designer)

Published by The Goldberg Agency
@Almostabook

Library of Congress Cataloging -in Publication-Data
Names: Goldberg, Seth - Author / Stone, Stephen - Illustrator
Title: The Book of Almosts, Nice Tries, and Good Attempts: Tall Tales with Epic Fails,
written by Seth Goldberg, illustrated by Stephen Stone.

ISBN 979-8-218-11347-6 (hbk)
ISBN 979-8-218-11314-8 (pbk)

Display type set in Goby/Tobi
Text type set in Tobi Pro/Light
Art Direction by Seth Goldberg

DEDICATION

To the subversive comedians and humorists who inspire me—the ones who made me and continue to make me laugh and think.

To my father, who taught me about word economy, an example being the time he ended up in a hospital with an oxygen level "inconsistent with life," as his doctor put it. I was there when the poor nurse came in and asked, "How are you feeling today, Mr. Goldberg?" assuming (or at least hoping) she'd get the standard and generally inoffensive, "Fine. Thank you." His response? "Indignant," which is how he genuinely felt. I believe that was the last time anyone checked in on him.

To my mother, who would gleefully make the most cringeworthy puns, each of which I pretended pained me to hear. On that note, I may have inadvertently (or purposely) slipped a couple of my own into this book. Prepare to cringe, in jest or for real.

To my brother, whose voice I heard in the back of my head while writing this book. It often asked me in a declarative way, "You realize this book sucks, right?" which motivated me to take additional passes at each story to find ways to improve them. In truth, when I told my most unfiltered critic I planned to write a book of comedy, he straight up said, "You should be good at that." Who knows what he thinks now?

To Al and cousin Sue. Just because Sue wanted a shout out.

Finally, to my teenage son—the college student. Not long ago, he was the poor soul who read sixty of my short stories, gently giving me a thumbs down on over two-thirds of them. "Ehhh" or "Not your best stuff, Dad" were common refrains. But on those occasions when he laughed out loud while reading, I knew I'd struck gold (or was at least digging in the right mine). Thanks kiddo. I love you.

The BOOK of Almosts, Nice Tries, and Good Attempts

by
Seth Goldberg

Illustrated by
Stephen Stone

PREFACE

The Fellow Who Retired and Resolved to Be Unproductive

I don't cook. Despite my soft skin, I'm not pretty enough to model. "What am I equipped to do now?" I wondered after folding my company in late 2020. "What do I want to do?" I had the same simple answer to both questions: nothing. After working nonstop for thirty years, it was time to be unproductive.

Some people won't brag about things like: (1) not getting up to find a remote control or (2) ordering in food versus whipping up a meal. But I did … to anyone who would listen. I was proud to be unproductive and living my dream. Yet right when I started to find my groove, 2022 intervened. "As you're breathing again without your negative-ion necklace—the one that *magically* fought off Covid, it's time you found a new challenge," she insisted. 2022 was right … and a bit of a douche.

"I can relearn Chinese!" I decided. A big hit at law school in Shanghai, China, I'd rebuild the skill which endeared me to Chinese waiters everywhere. That plan died quickly. Too much thinking, too soon. "I can throw a résumé out there and see what hits!" was my next inclination. But I don't want a boss. And if memory serves me, I tend not to be their favorite employee either. Then I recalled that in 2001, I wrote elements of a book I never bothered to finish. "That's it!" I exclaimed, not realizing it would have helped to have had my next thought ready. Then it hit me. It was time to revisit my collection of stories.

The Book of Almosts, Nice Tries, and Good Attempts is an homage to everyone looking for a purpose; who dreams of pushing beyond their limitations; who is compelled to do what in their heart feels right, only to fall flat on their face. That's what this book is … me face planting. I hope you enjoy.

QUAD
LATTE

CONTENTS

CONTENTS

There's Something Suspicious about Less than Three Wishes

Martin Blonski knew the rules. His genie had made sure of it by placing them in the welcome package. But there was really just one of any importance: *only two wishes per customer.* Prior owners had been okay with it (other than one old man, who, to read his own welcome letter, had wished for better lighting and a larger font). But it was clear to Martin he was getting a raw deal.

It shouldn't have mattered. Martin already had it all—a beautiful wife, his own electric sausage grinder, and two and a half wonderful children (one of them was kind of meh). He had no need for wishes. But when an antique lamp turns up in your attic, you're going to have certain expectations, and if offered fewer than the standard three wishes, you'll fight like heck to get a third … just on principle.

And that was Martin in a word: *principled.* He preferred that to his six-word description: *the chubby guy with a mustache* (a label he'd been tagged with since the end of second grade). Yet the way others viewed him was not the issue. The question was how to snag his desired extra wish.

Martin read through the genie handbook (the dusty one in his attic). There was nothing on wishes that guaranteed three. He called Genie Customer Service to explain his frustration. No genie could help him. Not one of them was free. The more Martin tried, the more he failed. He'd be granted two wishes or none at all. He chose none—but he got even.

Each day, for the rest of his life, Martin brought meals to the genie in his attic, but not dinner. The genie expected the standard three meals, but like Martin's third wish, it was never guaranteed.

MAY
1990-95
DIRTY MAGS
BEST AT FINDING LAMPS
GENIE HANDBOOK
100 POLISH JOKES
MAKING AMENDS with
YOUR POLISH OWNER
ANTIQUE
BOOKS
TODAY'S
MENU
BREAKFAST
- EGGS
LUNCH
- TUNA
DINNER
- NOT
HAPPENING!

Nearly an Astronaut

Every so often, someone remarkable inspires us to dream big, showing us by example that anything is possible. "Rocketman" Rob Reinhart was not that person. A would-be astronaut, he lacked any sense of direction, other than simply knowing what he wanted to be.

He came into this world on a cold Christmas morning, at a hospital not far from where his mother gave birth.[1] Eventually retrieved, he spent most of his childhood building model rockets, all of which flew sideways. Yet he never lost his spirit. After all, above him was a galaxy full of mystery and adventure, and if he turned enough ways, perhaps he'd see it.

As for getting to space, of course, that's what he wanted. Had you asked him, he'd have told you it was always on his mind. Although, it was much more likely he'd see snow in the summer, or his dad would come home after "buying his pack of cigarettes," neither of which was going to happen.

"If only there weren't so many directions," he'd often lament. "I could probably handle one or two." But for a guy who still couldn't work a zipper, even that was optimistic.

Rob never stopped dreaming he'd explore the stars. Yet, he never became an astronaut. He would have been perfect for the job … had he not lacked every skill needed to succeed. But with his Midwest charm, his knack for fitting comfortably into body-encasing clothing, and his propensity to plant American flags in unexpected places, he was the next best thing.

Years later, after significant directional therapy, things began looking up for Rob Reinhart, most notably his eyes.

[1] In other words, he's so bad at directions that he even popped out at the wrong facility. Try and keep up here.

MARS OR BUST
ASA
ROCKETMAN
ALIEN SPACESHIP
PRETEND ASTRONAUT
ALBUQUERQUE 200 MI
ROB'S PARKED CAR
SOMEONE'S WALLET
I ♥ COWS

The Girl Who Refused to Be Amused

There was tension in the waiting room as the young couple huddled, anxious for word on the doctor's finding. Then it came. Their daughter, Molly, had been born with a serious disposition. The tests were conclusive. She scowled at peekaboo and sneered at anyone foolish enough to pull an errant quarter from behind her ear. She didn't like those things or anything else. Molly simply refused to be amused.

But her parents wouldn't accept it. When she got older, they hired handymen with tall ladders to clean the gutters near her bedroom window, only to yell, "Whoa. Whoa. Whoa!!!" as they'd fall backward into the pool. Molly saw them and frowned. Her dad would purposely leave for work with no pants on, her mom with toilet paper stuck to her shoe. Molly didn't care.

Desperate to see her smile, they even bought her a pony—a Shetland with a delightful demeanor ... who hatched a plan to get hit by a bus within minutes of meeting Molly. She dragged everything happy down into her orbit. It was an instantly isolating place to be.

Her parents were out of options ... until they learned about a surgeon and the transplant procedure she offered to girls bereft of humor. A long shot? Maybe. Worth trying? For sure. So, they sat Molly down to explain the opportunity, along with all the inherent risks, and she laughed at the two of them for being idiots ... and they lived happily ever after.

HANDY BRO'S
LIZARD CANNON
DO NOT USE CHICKENS
HANDY BRO'S

The Thief Who Couldn't Get Picked Out of a Lineup

It always bothered petty thief Peter Pilfor that no one paid him much attention.

I DID IT!
DO NOT TAP ON GLASS!
DO NOT TAP ON OFFICER
WORLDS BEST COP
POLICE
6'0"
5'6"
5'0"
4'6"
4'0"
6'0"
5'6"
5'0"
4'6"
4'0"
3'6"

The Pirate Who Lost His Way

The map he was holding was precisely drawn, as was each one before it.

Take ten steps toward the coconut tree. Turn right. Walk to the guy in the grayish-blue swim trunks who's staring at the woman that isn't his wife. Clear his table of plates and utensils, then place them in the sink.

The instructions were easy for Captain Edwin Edwards, a busboy at Tom's Beachside Delights. After all, maps were kind of his thing.

Once a feared pirate, notorious both for his brutality and for being the guy who wrongly insisted there are six, not seven, seas, Captain Ed had long since hit rock bottom. His malnourished parrot was clear-cut proof. "Polly want anything," she'd whimper, sensing her poverty. "But how to get more money?" Ed wondered. He couldn't pillage his table sections. Only senior management was allowed to plunder. He couldn't dig up his hidden treasure. Valet had sailed away with his ship. "Everyone dumps on you, don't they?" asked Polly while relieving herself. "You're right," said Ed. "It's time I make a stand." (An ironic statement from a man who would have been one had he one more wooden leg!)

Desperate to grow his savings, Captain Ed took a stab at being a server. He did poorly, however, and made all the usual pirate mistakes. He buried coins used as payment rather than put them in the cashbox. He'd yell, "I'm a captain! I don't *take* orders!" when anyone dared to ask for food. Ill-suited to serve and a pirate at heart, he made off with the register. But without a map, he just looped his way back before anyone saw it was gone.

TOM'S
BEACHSIDE
Delights
ED'S

The Second Fastest Gun in the West

There were a lot of gunslingers in the untamed West—and a handful of great ones. Johnny "Pretty Sure Thing" McGraw was the best of them all. Almost.

Having graduated first in his class at Gunfighter College, the only school to offer a duel degree program, he was, undoubtedly, a top-notch marksman. And there were things he could do with a Colt .45 that no one had ever seen. He could split a hair at twenty paces. A fine skill, all agreed, but useless against a killer who'd gone prematurely bald … and "Handsome" Hank Henderson was that and more.

Of course, in a gunfight, there'd be other places to aim, like at Hank's perfect teeth or his crystal-blue eyes. (Johnny wouldn't have to take a hair shot.) But when the two met up in the streets of Oklahoma City, in what the posters all billed as the "Showdown in O' Town," it didn't matter which part of Hank Johnny was targeting, because he never got off a shot.

The coroner approached to measure Johnny for a coffin. And he saw Hank had hit him in the head, the heart, and every other body part that began with an *h* as was his signature. As for "Handsome" Hank Henderson, that day marked a turning point. It was the last time he would fire a gun … at Johnny "Pretty Sure Thing" McGraw.

BURY & SONS
SALOON
BUY ONE GET ONE FREE!
HERE LIES
SHOWDOWN IN O' TOWN
OKLAHOMA

The Guy Whose Writing Was Far from Exciting

Aspiring author Billy Badger wasn't particularly talented. Yet, his writing was colorful … thanks to his prolific use of crayons. And that was all it took to get people talking.

That included the crowd at his local coffee shop, all of whom seemed to adore him. "Billy's here!" they'd yell whenever he walked in. They wouldn't yell like that to the other authors who wrote there. Of course, none of them were named Billy.

Despite never having finished any works he'd started, Billy fashioned himself to be a serious writer—the kind who could walk into a room buzzing with intellectuals and hear things whispered like, "That's the guy I was telling you about," or, "I keep some of his writing taped to my refrigerator. It brightens up my kitchen!" In Billy's mind, to gain respect as an author, getting noticed was half the battle. As for the other half, he was totally unarmed.

To sample his work, you'd need only read his novel—at least the part that had been written. Just three chapters long, it was already a page-turner. Read a page and you'd rush to the next one, desperately praying it would somehow be better. It never was.

"I can do this!" Billy would say. He didn't lack confidence, and he didn't know the meaning of the word *impossible*. "Oh," he said after looking it up. "That's what it means."

Years later, after selling no copies of his semi-conceived works, Billy accepted he wasn't really an author. But with a pretend publisher always seated nearby, he couldn't give up on the ruse.

Take a Compliment
Its free
CLOSED
RACE IS AN ILLUSION
But Prices here aren't
You're nice!
10 WAYS TO FORGET YOUR EX
PUBLISHER
INBOX
B
B

Nearly a Native American Legend

He wasn't the most feared Sioux warrior. He'd never taken a scalp during battle or driven the white man off his tribal lands. That wasn't his style. It was also true that the other warriors didn't want him around—not after the last war, when he accidentally fought for the wrong side. But when Wandering Mind settled down to start a family, he showed them all how to keep the peace.

His wife adored him. How couldn't she? Would another man sit still for his wife while she dished on all the latest dirt? Unlikely, unless he worked the fields, where knowing dirt trends is useful, or could tune her out like Wandering Mind. His blank stare, which she mistook for an admiring gaze, was the highlight of her every morning. Their children adored him too. His son practiced rattling, his daughter, dancing, and always there was their doting dad. He'd be thinking about things like the leaf he'd found earlier and how it resembled his chicken dinner, but no matter. His family felt loved, and so did he.

Tragically, Wandering Mind was struck by a tomahawk before his thirtieth birthday. It pierced his skull between the eyes, disrupting pizza night and leading to his death. He would have been fine … had he instead grabbed a buffalo tail to swat the fly on his forehead, but his mind was elsewhere. It always was.

"How?" he asked, his spirit fading. But with the word meaning *hello* in his native Lakota, everyone just waved back.

USE for FLIES
USE for BATTLE
TODAYS TOP SOIL
SIOUX SILT
PIZZA TEEPEE

An Almost Epic Music Festival

Her grandmother dropped acid at Woodstock. Her father picked up syphilis in the bleachers at Live Aid. They were free spirits who, like Miriam, loved music and inspired the festival she proudly pioneered.

What she'd organized was, for the most part, beyond impressive. After confirming it wouldn't be used that weekend, she booked Rhode Island as the event site. For the teens she bought fireworks, custom explosions in the form of trending memes. Miriam even found a charity, Save the Kids Who We Didn't Have a Chance to Save Last Time at a Totally Unrelated Concert, to which she funneled some of the proceeds. But she didn't deliver on the main thing promised: the music.

She did book acts. That wasn't the issue. The problem was none of them had the means to entertain.

There was a band made up entirely of toddlers. For an hour they banged their spoons on a plate, which wasn't much to hear. But it got them fed.

There was a well-known actress, who was convinced she was a singer. But those who heard her "sing" were far less persuaded. (A child in the audience thought she might have been an airplane, when she took off before he could get her autograph. No one mistook her for an actual musician.)

Not even a Ramones reunion could fire up the crowd. Miriam helped them reunite (she thought for a performance) after hearing they used to be a great live band—unaware that they used to be an alive band as well.[2] Nothing went right. The festival floundered.

The next year, Miriam tried yet again, with effort to avoid her past mistakes. And with her grandmother checking each artist for a pulse, it was at least a better start.

---

[2] Sadly, all four of the original band members have passed away.

JOEY
TOMMY
JOHNNY
DEE DEE
PICTURES
WITH BAND
$5.00
SAVE the KIDS

The Guy Who Built the Other Ark

His name was Todd, and the Lord never liked him. He'd even forgotten Todd was alive and why He'd bothered to furnish him with shelter when Todd, like his neighbors, was set to drown. After all, he was wicked, and the wicked were doomed. Only Noah had an ark to survive the flood; that is, until Todd built his. Not because he feared some approaching Armageddon. He was just super competitive.

Known in the neighborhood for being a three-time district wrestling champion and a perennial all-star at sticks and stones, Todd refused to let anyone steal his spotlight. That included his daughter—whose lemonade stand had once brought joy to their community, until it mysteriously succumbed to fire … five times.

But when Todd met Noah, he'd met his match. "The old man thinks he can build the best ark in town," Todd had told himself dismissively (after Noah had informed him of his grand ambition). Now, many years later, the world would decide.

The initial advantage went to Todd. When Noah built his ark 300 cubits long, Todd built his to 301. When Noah assembled every animal, female and male, aboard his ark, Todd did the same … then topped him with a set that was gender fluid. He outdid Noah at every turn, but his fortunes changed when the rain waters fell.

Fights broke out in the galley of Todd's ark after a llama misspoke and called a "they" a "she" (simply because they seemed to overthink things and couldn't parallel park). And when the tussling animals capsized his ark, Todd realized he'd lost and that name tags may have helped.

TODD
MRS
MR
200
250
300
250
3 +1

The Man Who Inspired the Legend of Tarzan. Almost

He knew from the moment he picked up the book that what he was reading was his own life story. The similarities were uncanny—the action, the romance. Somehow, while sculpting his tales of Tarzan, Edgar Rice Burroughs had drawn on each meaningful moment from John Harrington's time in equatorial Africa. But how? They'd never met, and there was no written account of John's stay on the continent.

Tarzan *was* John, with only minor embellishments.

Tarzan was prone to travel the jungle by swinging on vines from tree to tree.

John Harrington was more a walker than a swinger and stuck to cafés and outdoor markets.

Tarzan had a chilling, yodel-like scream he used to summon the beasts of the jungle.

John Harrington didn't so much scream as bark: at his girlfriend for wasting his money on trinkets and their tour guide for moving at too brisk a pace.

But Harrington's pain is what Burroughs captured so poignantly.

Tarzan was battered in a life-or-death fight with an ape he killed with his own bare hands.

John Harrington was crushed—effectively dead to the girlfriend who ditched him for a fast-walking tour guide.

In the end, John conceded that while there were certainly similarities, he might not have been the model for Tarzan. That it was written in 1912 and his cruise to West Africa was in 2020 should have been his first clue. Then again, he wasn't Sherlock Holmes either.

CLOSED
SOUVENIRS
SOLD OUT
Thanks JOHN!
SCARVES
TARZAN
DISCOVER the CONGO!
MINUTE TOURS
JUNGLE SAFARI SALE
MAPS

The Man Who Sat behind Lincoln's Hat

He thought about throwing a shoe at it to knock it off Lincoln's head, but his wife advised against it. What else could Victor Goldsmith do? Here he was at his very first play, and a big black hat was blocking his view.

"Why wear a hat to a theater?" he wondered. "Does its weight stop Lincoln from floating away?" (He was, after all, exceptionally thin.) Victor had to assume Lincoln was just being a dick.

And Victor was right. When he bobbed, Lincoln weaved. When he stood, Lincoln stretched. Wherever he moved, Lincoln blocked him at every turn. Short on options, he yelled, "Look! Over there! Slaves!" But Lincoln didn't flinch. He knew they'd been emancipated. Victor even paid an usher to tell the president there was a call for him in the lobby. That failed too, as the telephone was still a decade from invention. His wife urged patience as she scribbled "iPhone" on her shopping list.

No matter what he tried, no matter the plan, Victor couldn't stop Lincoln from doing his antics. Then John Wilkes Booth took a shot in the dark and managed to find a way. Victor wondered, "What play did he miss because of that asshole Lincoln? Must have been a good one." Except it wasn't. It was Cats.

And that was the last time Victor would step inside a theater … unarmed.

GENERAL SEATING
PRESIDENTS TOO
HANG IN THERE

The Woman Who Claimed to Have Exact Change

It had been a quiet day at the Speed Mart supermarket. There hadn't been so much as an inconvenient spill … until Nancy Nieman got to the register and sent shock waves through the store. "I'll pay in cash, and I have exact change!" she declared (to a cashier who hadn't yet decided what to make of her). And suddenly, things got interesting.

There had been only one other instance, in the store's entire history, where a woman had claimed she had exact change. And that dated back to the early 1980s. It was easy for shoppers to describe her in detail. She was still in the queue at checkout line four.

Nancy wasn't deterred … not even after she looked in her purse and realized it was empty. Her mother had taught her the importance of perseverance (just days before giving up on her). There was no way Nancy would give up without a fight.

That was bad news for those who were waiting in line behind her. They had hoped she'd pay so they could too. But when she spent the next hour combing through her bag, sharing photos of her children along the way, they came to understand they were not her concern.

What mattered to Nancy? Finding change.

She checked the coin machine by the bathroom, the floor of her car, and every one of her pockets. Nada. She even rummaged through a stranger's pocket, which was awkward because his wife was looking there too. Neither found a penny. Nancy still had nothing.

Tired and ready to admit defeat, Nancy offered to pay with plastic. But with everyone having gone home for the night, no one could pretend to care.

"This is a photo of my youngest, Jason," Nancy told the cashier, feigning humility. "What a lovely boy," was the equally ingenuine response.

Jacques in the Box and Can't Get Out

He'd once escaped from an imaginary straitjacket in under twenty-three seconds, at the time a mime record. This should have been a cakewalk for Jacques Le Souffle. As easy as pie. And yet, here he was, in a make-believe box, locked inside with no obvious way out.

For years he'd believed he couldn't be boxed in. Pantomime, imitation … he could do it all. But somehow today, as he peered through each wall of his imagined enclosure, he saw everything but options.

Flanking and ignoring him as they toppled his empty tip can were musicians, dancers, and other admired street performers. Tourists brushed by him without a hint of concern. His predicament? They noticed it, as did everyone in or passing through the plaza. But per tradition dating back to the early nineteenth century, when a mime first appeared on the streets of France, no one gave a shit about Jacques or his situation.

Of course, those people avoiding him couldn't help Jacques. What he needed was someone who knew the ropes. Not the pretend ones he pulled on to make his way around the plaza, but rather, the proper methods to free a mime. His assistant would do. She couldn't be found. Like his options and his social life, she didn't exist.

Later that evening, after hours of humiliation, the mime union came and set him free, burning through countless imaginary chain saws in the process. None of them ever spoke a word about that day, or anything else.

DO NOT
FEED THE
MIMES
PANTO PIAZZA
SUPPORT
FREE
SPEECH!

The Second Person to Discover Fire

He was so excited by his big discovery he dropped his stone and ran to the cave. "Look what Kron find!" shouted Kron to anyone who'd listen, as he held up a stick engulfed in flames. "Me find it in woods. Kron hurts when he touch."

"Sticks sometimes sharp," noted his good friend Torc, yet again displaying his encyclopedic knowledge of all ten things known to mankind. "Take care with stick."

But that's not what Kron meant. (Besides, Kron knew about sticks, and how sharp they often were. The ones still lodged in him served as a reminder.)

He clarified, "Kron mean *burny stuff* on *top* of stick." The burny stuff being what he called the flames.

"Oh … Kron means *fire*," said Torc, now understanding. "Mokrak already have."

"How Mokrak have what me just discover?" Kron wondered. Had he, like Kron, been hit by lightning while peeing on a tree from its highest perch? Perhaps, but Kron couldn't confirm until he reached his cave. Even a Neanderthal could smell trouble coming … or at minimum, something cooking.

As Kron had feared, when they entered the cave, there was a burger waiting for him and Torc. "Hope you no mind lamb burger," said Mokrak sheepishly.[3] "Cow hide outside cave."

Kron grabbed at the flames beneath Mokrak's grill. They burned his hands, like the burny stuff on his stick. "Damn," sighed Kron, acknowledging the hard truth. "Mokrak find fire first."

Two weeks later, Kron invented the wheel. But with his scientific credentials now under scrutiny, no one really cared.

---

[3] You found this dad joke to be especially painful. I'm well aware.

WIPE YOUR FEET
BEFORE ENTERING
CAVE
BURNY STUFF
Grill MASTER

The Man Who Had to Escape His Escape Room

In retrospect, the arrow-themed wall design may not have been ideal for an escape room—not with each arrow pointing at a large rolling armoire and the exit hidden behind it. Could that have been the reason for the iffy online reviews? "Perhaps," thought Jimmy, the venue's owner and designer. But as a claustrophobe, he was disposed to making exits accessible.

The only thing striking about the place is the low overhead fan. That left quite an impression, mostly on my forehead ...

The Easy Way Out escape room was a godsend to those on tight schedules and anyone loathing a long night out. Designed with the person who didn't want to be there in mind, it ensured a fast escape. Most time consuming was your choice to follow either the arrows, the pirate-style map on the floor, or the voice calling out from behind the armoire, yelling, "This way! I wouldn't lie to you! And I have pie too!" (That last part wasn't true.) No riddles to solve, no cleverly hidden keys ... The challenge was finding something to do before finding yourself back out on the street. That took talent.

The sign out front read. "Easy Way Out Escape Room." I should have paid closer attention. Imagine if it had said, "Free Colonoscopies." But I wouldn't stand for that.

Sadly, within its first week of opening, Easy Way Out was forced to close its doors. That meant anyone escaping now had to open each door themselves. Jimmy found it stifling and sold his business, leaving nearly as fast as his paying customers.

I hate my husband's friends. This place was perfect! In what seemed like seconds we were on our way home.

Is that my MAP?
NO CLUES HERE
DON'T TAKE
IT WON'T HELP
THERE BE NOTHING HERE
Arggh! WRONG WAY

Almost a Superhero

By day, he was Doug Richards; a seemingly ordinary man who worked assembly line four at the Sit and Spin Stool factory. At night, he was still just Doug. But by then he'd be home, eating pretzels on his sofa. He left it to his coworkers Rainmaker, Fireball, and the Velvet Touch to fight evil, because unfortunately for Doug, he had no special power.

Sure, it was great he arrived on time for everything, but that wasn't magic. Nor was his ability to say the perfect thing whenever someone passed away. "Barry had big feet," Doug remarked to Barry's widow not two weeks earlier. His words eased her pain … reminding her how when she'd tied his shoes, he'd flash a smile with his freakishly large teeth. None of it mattered. Until Doug could jump a building, bend steel, or find the safe answer to "Does this make me look fat?" he wouldn't be certified superhuman.

Each evening, in the quiet of his apartment, Doug prayed he'd receive an exceptional ability. What it was didn't matter. It could have been a power that no one would wish for, like being able to summon fish or to assume the form of water. He'd take it. He just wanted the tools to be part of a team.

Sadly for Doug, he simply wasn't super. Like his friend Marvin Davis, a.k.a. Dream Catcher, who liked to walk through theaters and wake anyone sleeping, and his ex, Lady Intuition, who sensed she had abilities but couldn't name a single one, he did not register on the "super" spectrum.

In time, and after further self-reflection, Doug let go of his superhero ambitions. Having saved several comrades in Desert Storm and twice delivered a baby on a plane, each of which was on fire (not the babies, the planes), he could live with being just a model citizen.

MINUTES WITHOUT AN ACCIDENT
15
ON TIME RECORD
JAN Doug
FEB Doug
MAR Doug
APR Doug
MAY Doug
JUN
JUL
AUG
SEPT
OCT
NOV
DEC
SUPER HERO CHANGING ROOM
SUPER HERO CHANGING ROOM
NO DOUGS
NO. 4
DOUG

Nearly the New Guy at a Restricted Club

Love your neighbors. Build bridges over every divide. It's a noble sentiment. But it's a challenge when you're unliked because of how you were born, or what you believe.

So, when applicant Haim Lefkowitz was asked to join the exclusive We Don't Want You society in East Hampton, New York, he was thrilled but bewildered.

Was his religion not clear to them? He marked the "Other" box where the application prompted him to respond with either that or "Very, Very White and Not Jewish." He'd sent in the requested picture of his circumcision, which unbeknownst to him, he was the first to supply. He even botched the two questions specifically designed to trip up Jews: "Which would you use: a nail or a screw?" (fix-it-up work is Jewish kryptonite) and "Name the Best Athlete Ever" (if you named a Jew, you'd be wrong).[4] Haim fell for every trick and stepped in every trap, but they still were ready to take him in. "Maybe the gentleman who emailed me the forms enjoyed kibbitzing over the phone?" Haim wondered. It was only a theory.

Initiation day came. Haim skipped it to make the minyan at his nephew's bar mitzvah—which finally made clear to We Don't Want You members he wasn't one of them. (Somehow, his nonstop kvetching about the temperature in their lobby hadn't been a tip-off.)

Uninvited to be a member but undeterred, he got them to join his temple. He just told them its name was the "No Jews" club to get them to apply.

---

[4] To clarify for those who are curious, despite some of the write-in answers provided by Italians seeking membership, "nails" are what you hit with a hammer. And, apparently, there are better athletes than Sandy Koufax, the phenomenal Jewish Major League Baseball pitcher from the 1950s and '60s, who many Jews revere as the best athlete ever!

בֵּית כְּנֶסֶת
NOAH & TODD GENESIS 6:9-22
WELCOME TO ALL OUR
JEWISH MEMBERS
KVETCHING
TOURNAMENT
THIS WEDNESDAY

COMMUNITY
MEET & GREET
INVOICE
BILL

ALL ARE
WELCOME
TOM'S
BEACHSIDE
Delights

Background & Musings on Each Story

In my directions to the illustrator, Stephen Stone, I never specified a race for my main character, Martin. Steve came back to me with his early sketches, letting me know he made Martin Polish. Fine. No problem. Then I smelled opportunity to milk it. I changed his last name to Blonski (from an earlier, generic last name). I also added a couple of titles to the bookcase holding all of the "antique books." The first one was 100 Polish Jokes, an out-of-favor title, similar to others you might have found at the bookstore in the 1970s. Then I thought … if this genie has a Polish jokebook that he's obviously using to get under Martin's skin, then he'll need a way back into Martin's good graces—assuming he wants to eat. That's why the book underneath it is *Making Amends with Your Polish Owner.*

True Story: As a kid, I used to buy those jokebooks. I thought they were funny. The classic (and, perhaps, least inspired) joke being:

Q: How many Polish people does it take to change a light bulb?

A: Five. One to hold the bulb and four to turn the ladder.

What did all of the jokes have in common? None of them painted a flattering picture of the Polish people. One day my dad says to me, "You realize your grandparents are from Poland, and you're part Polish?" Well *fuck* me. Who knew? As a result of receiving that important information, a few years later, I stopped telling Polish jokes.

ON: Almost an Astronaut

My son came up with the twist for this story. I was brainstorming ideas, and I decided to write about an astronaut. But I needed a hook. I asked my son for input. He said, "What if this guy has no sense of direction?" "I love it," I told him. "Now get out of here and do homework or something."

Regarding the illustration, there was one joke I elected to not include. I can lie and say I was worried that it was too crude and that I didn't want to offend anyone. But I'm okay with things like that. Truth is, I was more concerned that I'd be the only person to get the joke. See the girl on her father's shoulders? Her hat says, "I HEART Cows." Her dad (the farmer) has a hat too. There's nothing on it. I wanted to put "I HEART Sheep" there, thinking, "Who doesn't love a good joke about bestiality?"

Looking back on it now, it was a missed opportunity.

ON: The Girl Who Refused to Be Amused

About the illustration: You're probably wondering, "Why shouldn't I place a chicken in a lizard cannon?" It's an intriguing question. Right? The answer is simple.

You shouldn't put a chicken in a lizard cannon because unlike chickens, lizards are naturals at handling the spotlight. Look at that lizard in the illustration. He's a born entertainer. With the chicken, you're getting a wild card. Can anyone say with confidence he'll make Molly laugh? To my mind, that chicken could easily run afowl of expectations.

Sorry. That came to mind, and I couldn't stop myself.

ON: The Thief Who Couldn't Get Picked Out of a Lineup

Yeah. I went there. And of course, me being me, as soon as I came up with the idea for the illustration, I shared it with *all* of my black friends.

He thought it was funny … Actually, this fellow more precisely said, "You're an asshole … Only you." Then he laughed his ass off.

I still haven't shown this illustration to one of my oldest and dearest friends (yes, black, and a very successful physician). He'll understand it's not the doctor getting ribbed. If we're judging anyone, it's people who are blinded by personal prejudice … and old ladies. I fucking hate old ladies.

Not really. Anyways, this gal clearly missed an obvious sign that her pick was wrong.

As for my friend, the doctor … he's known me long enough to be aware I have no animus toward any group of people. There may be a few, individual representatives of many groups that I don't care for. That's a separate discussion.

ON: The Pirate Who Lost His Way

I almost called this story, "The Pirate Who Couldn't Get Back on His Feet." I mean, it's about a guy who used to be a big-time pirate, now stuck on land and bussing tables. Plus, he has two wooden legs. Great title. Right?

Meanwhile, when I decided to do a pirate story, I initially leaned toward something in the way of "The Pirate Who Couldn't Walk the Plank."

It would begin with a crew that had recently mutinied. They'd put their captain on the plank, only to watch him run and then jump into the water. The next time they put him up there, he'd cartwheel off the plank, then roller skate, jetpack, and so on and so forth. The result would always be that they pull him out of the water and force him to do it again, until he can figure out how to correctly *walk* a plank. Maybe some of the crew, trying to be helpful, walk the plank into shark-infested waters—just to illustrate proper form. (Of course, in their case, they would each perish.) The captain would see their example, give everyone the thumbs-up, try again, but still get it wrong.

Damn it. I ran with the wrong story.

ON: The Second Fastest Gun in the West

Of all the stories I wrote back in 2001 (and I wrote about twenty of them), "The Second Fastest Gun in the West" was the only one strong enough to use in this book. Consider that. I wrote twenty stories, thought they were all wonderful, put them in a box, opened the box over twenty years later, and then realized nineteen of them sucked. At the very least, they weren't good enough to use, and couldn't be salvaged.

Now imagine how I'm going to feel when I reread this book.

ON: The Guy Whose Writing Was Far from Exciting

I've never understood why at every coffee shop, so many people have a laptop. Is it, as I've guessed, to write the quintessential book or screenplay? That seems to be a common perception, and somewhat plausible.

I've also always assumed that you won't find any John Grishams tucked away in the corner of your local coffee shop. Rather, you're likely to encounter folks like our Billy—those who have the passion, but not necessarily the ability. On that note, I added myself into the illustration, sneaking my manuscript into the pseudo-publisher's inbox. It felt appropriate. Who knows if I'll sell more than a few copies of this book?

I'd probably buy it. Then again, I live alone, and I own five umbrellas. I'm clearly not the smartest shopper.

ON: Nearly a Native American Legend

I had fun writing this one. (I hated writing all of those other ones.) I wanted to tell a story about a guy who dreamt of being a superhero, which I later did. But as soon as I landed on the superhero name Wandering Mind, this story became one about a Native American. I couldn't ignore the possibilities—a Native American airhead who was consequently a great husband but a lousy warrior.

Do you like Grandpa? Wandering Mind has been dead for all of a few minutes, and Grandpa is already walking into the teepee, doing the "there's an arrow in my head" routine. Very Steve Martin of him (that was his *thing* for a while).

Just so you know, I did do a little homework for this one. The Lakota Sioux actually use the word *how* (or as it's properly spelled, *Háu*), to say hello. On the other hand, there is at least one item in the illustration that is factually incorrect. The Sioux may have been able to order in Chinese, but definitely not pizza.

ON: An Almost Epic Music Festival

About the illustration: If you're a fan of the Ramones, like I am, I hope you appreciate the punk element of their presentation. It's meant to be a little "in your face," which they and their music were too. I'd like to think they'd be amused by the joke and illustration. Just an amazing band, and it's a huge loss to no longer have them around.

As for the story … writing it was an educational experience. And the learning began after I asked myself a single, important question: Has anything ever happened in Rhode Island? Apparently, nothing has. I did months of research, but the state has no history. I couldn't find record of any residents. Even New Jersey has something to be proud about: Bruce Springsteen. It must make Rhode Island sad. As for the Griffins, they're not real. That was Rhode Island's last chance at relevance.

Best I can tell (after consulting a few historians who know very little, but for whom I have the utmost respect), Rhode Island remains a relatively small, uninhabited swath of land, and a great place to rent for parties and festivals.

And I'm all about having a great time.

ON: The Guy Who Built the Other Ark

I'm guessing there weren't many Jews around back in the days of Noah. "Why?" you ask. You see, if I were Noah's neighbor, and I saw him building an ark, and he told me there was a flood coming and we all were going to die, well sure … I'd think he was crazy. But I'd immediately start to build my own ark. Call it the Jewish survival instinct.

Here's how it works.

A Jew will automatically ask themself two questions when faced with a new or unfamiliar situation. The first is, "What can go wrong?" The second is, "How am I prepared?" They can be on their way to a friend's wedding. They'll ask those two questions. A Jew never says, "Wow! This is great!" or "Can you imagine the possibilities here?" That's how you know you're talking with a gentile.

With respect to Noah … the chance that he was right, and not crazy, was a million to one. As a Jew, I'd have zeroed in on that "one" possibility. I would have pulled out my tools (a.k.a. hired a neighbor) and built an ark, even if it cut into the time I usually allocate to complaining and some of my other hobbies. At the end of the day, I'd rather be tired from managing someone else's hard work than treading water.

And that's why I doubt there were Jews other than Noah. He had the only ark in town.

ON: The Man Who Inspired the Legend of Tarzan … Almost

Cool fact about this story … at least cool to me. After I wrote it, a question occurred to me. (That's not the cool part. What follows is.) I wondered if alluding to the character Tarzan could be problematic. I read up on it a bit and confirmed that the estate of Edgar Rice Burroughs had maintained certain legal rights to it. I'm not sure they would have been sufficient to prevent me from using it as I do (I'm not an expert in the area), but I knew if they were so inclined, they could have, at the very least, made my life difficult.

I reached out to them to confirm whether they saw my use as problematic. No answer. I tried a second and, I presumed, final time. I figured, "What more can I do?" Then a funny thing happened. They read my story and got back to me. We worked it out for me to get their go-ahead to run with the story, as is. That was pretty cool. I told myself that because they hadn't raised objection, they must not have hated it. Then again, I often pull compliments out of thin air.

By the way … a fast-walking tour guide whose company is called Minute Tours and whose logo is a minotaur? Pretty clever, right? Fine. Whatever.

ON: The Man Who Sat behind Lincoln's Hat

I'll tell you how I came up with the concept. I was looking for tropes. I thought, what about Lincoln? Okay. So, what about him? Well, he's tall. Right? So, why should it matter? Well, if he's tall, maybe he tends to block the view of the people behind him. Okay. And where would that present the greatest issue? A theater, I decided. And of course, if you think of Lincoln in a theater, you'll go right to that tragic day when the man was assassinated. What could be funnier? So, I wrote the story.

Two months later, I'm watching an animated show about a family guy, and I see a cutaway with some fellow in a theater sitting behind Lincoln. He can't see past him and that big black hat. "Damn," I thought. Now someone is going to claim that I hadn't come up with the idea on my own. That bothered me … until two months later, when I saw another episode of the same show. It ran a different cutaway with Lincoln, in a theater, blocking somebody's view. This time, it was John Wilkes Booth who couldn't see the play. That's when I realized—if the show's own writers are independently coming up with similar concepts (I assume), then no one can challenge the pedigree of my story!

Perhaps they can say that it was too obvious a joke. (People can be mean like that.) But at least they can't claim I stole the idea.

My favorite element of the illustration is the sign on the wall: "General Seating—Presidents Too." I've never seen *that* in any animated television show … at least not yet.

ON: The Woman Who Claimed to Have Exact Change

So maybe this happens to you as well. You go to the supermarket and pick out your items. Then you head to the checkout, where you see two lines: one line has eight or so people in it, with carts full of products; the other has just one woman who looks ready to pay. I used to go to the shorter line, thinking it would be quicker. Then I learned.

So, what inevitably happens in that one-woman line? Well, the first thing is that despite physical cash being all but antiquated, she always wants to pay with it (versus using the twelve credit cards in her wallet). At some point, as the woman searches through her purse, rather than urge her to proceed with haste, the cashier inevitably asks her, "Would you like to join our frequent-shopper program?"

And it's never a yes or no answer. That would be too easy.

It's always something like, "Can you tell me more about the benefits?" Anyways, the circus usually continues for another ten or fifteen minutes. Meanwhile (when I used to get stuck in those lines), I'd open up my folding chair, make myself comfortable, and pass the time watching shoppers in the other line pay for their items and head out the door.

"Did the waiting bother you?" you ask. Actually, I haven't given it a second thought.

ON: Jacques in the Box and Can't Get Out

I believe this one might be Stephen's favorite illustration of the lot. He did come up with some amazingly clever elements for it. I told him I wanted a few mime firemen rushing onto the scene, carrying an imaginary ladder. He gave me that, but then put the shadow of the ladder on the wall behind them ... again, even though they weren't actually carrying one. I thought that was funny and a clever way to convey what they were pretending to carry. I also wanted a mime protestor protesting for free speech. Stephen put him out there in the plaza. But he drew him holding an imaginary pole for the sign pasted on the wall behind him. Again, nice way to show a mime miming. Thank you, Stephen.

ON: The Second Person to Discover Fire

I was afraid this story could bomb, given all of its caveman dialogue. But the first few people to whom I showed it seemed to like it. Even my editor got into the spirit of the story, offering me advice, such as, "I think a caveman would say it"—it being any number of things—"like this …"

Turns out that the change of pace on this story was refreshing … And I learned a lot about cavemen.

My favorite part of this illustration is the kid using Kron's stick with the burny stuff to cast a shadow on the wall, and the resulting dinosaur looking far more detailed than the kid's hand gestures should warrant. I was either going to go with the shadow-on-the-wall bit or present a caveman artist doing a portrait of a cavewoman. She'd have been quite homely. Our artist would have been carving her likeness into the wall, using only a stone. Yet, somehow, the resulting portrait would have borne more resemblance to a Botticelli than a creation resulting from stone-made markings.

That gag likely would have worked as well.

ON: The Man Who Had to Escape His Escape Room

I've never been to an escape room. I've seen the movie *Escape Room*. That didn't make me want to go to one. Anyways, I'm a bit claustrophobic. And the prospect of being locked in a room, with other people, upon whom I'm reliant to get out and go home, never held much allure to me. But I've wondered about escape rooms. And if I were to ever build one, I'd ensure that it presented no obstacles to finding the exit. You'd find it within seconds of entering the room. I'd probably call my establishment the Easy Way Out escape room.

At some point during the process of readying our illustrations, Stephen fell in love with our lizard daredevil (in case you haven't noticed). He even put him on the book cover. Here, yet again, he found way to incorporate him into an illustration—this time swinging from the blades of an overhead fan. I'm okay with it though. Let him have his fun.

I mean the lizard, of course. Stephen better get his ass back to his desk. I'm planning on doing a sequel to this book, and I can't do it without him.

ON: Almost a Superhero

We all want to be extraordinary. That's why I wrote this book. Not to be extraordinary ... but rather, as reminder that none of us are alone when it comes to coming up short.

Regarding the illustration, it provided loads of opportunities to throw in sight gags: the superhero changing room (a phone booth), the on-time record calendar, etc. But everything, including the story, began with me coming up with the names for my three superheroes: Rainmaker, Fireball, and the Velvet Touch. After that, I asked myself, "What could bring Doug and these three individuals together?" Then it became so obvious: they'd be making stools.

Now you know how stools are made.

ON: Nearly the New Guy at a Restricted Club

So, these types of clubs/societies do exist. Go out to the Hamptons, which is an area of Long Island, New York. You'll find clubs where people of particular religions and races remain unwelcome and unwanted. It kind of blew my mind the first time I went out there. How do these places still exist?

That's why I, being the great unifier that I am, thought to write a story where the goal was to bring people from different groups together. I hope it inspired you.

Assuming you read it, did you wonder what it means to "make the minyan"? It means you are the tenth adult to attend a Jewish religious service, thereby making it official. Really Jewish people allow only men to count. That's why really Jewish women shave their heads in protest … or something like that. I forget. It's been a while.

And then there's the story's ending. It struck me as pragmatic, despite the illustration. Obviously, putting the rabbi out front, at the top of the steps, should have set off alarm bells for the couple making their way inside. But every book deserves a happy ending.

THE END